C0-BOR-525

ROCKFORD PUBLIC LIBRARY
3 1112 01599000 1

WITHDRAWN

STORIES THE YEAR 'ROUND

"Turkey for Thanksgiving?" "No, Thanks!"

Alma Flor Ada

Illustrations by Vivi Escrivá

Translated from the Spanish by Rosa Zubizarreta

For Maikiko who loves to both listen to and create stories.

2105 N.W. 86th Ave.
Miami, FL 33122

09 08 07 06 05 4 5 6 7 8 9 10

Printed in Colombia

ISBN: 1-58105-224-3

It was a beautiful morning. After several days of rain, the sun had finally come out, and the rooster greeted him with a cheerful "Cock-a-doodle-doo!"

Everyone in the chicken yard — the rooster, the hens, the chickens, the ducks, the geese, and the turkey — was busy scratching for worms in the moist earth. The one who was finding the most worms and gulping them down the fastest was the turkey.

Gulping one worm after another, the turkey wandered closer and closer to the farm house. Since the kitchen window was open, he overheard a voice which said:

"Take a look at that turkey! Isn't he nice and plump? I bet he'll taste good at Thanksgiving dinner!"

"ME?" thought the turkey. "ME taste good? At Thanksgiving dinner?"

"I love turkey," said another voice, "especially when it's well-roasted to a nice golden-brown . . . You know I want you to save me a drumstick."

"He loves turkey, especially when it's well-roasted? ME well-roasted? He wants her to save him a drumstick? One of MY drumsticks?"

The turkey forgot all about scratching for worms. With his crest flopped over and his head hung low, he sunk deep in thought next to the great nut tree that grew in the middle of the chicken yard.

The turkey had been there for quite some time when he thought he heard a tiny voice. But the voice was so small and thin that the turkey wasn't sure whether he was really hearing something or only imagining it.

"What's wrong? What's the matter?" said the little voice. "Why are you so sad?"

"Who are you? Who is talking to me?" asked the turkey.

"Can't you see me? I'm right up here."

The turkey looked up and saw a beautiful spiderweb upon which a few drops of dew still shone. Right in the middle of the spiderweb sat a tiny spider.

"Why are you so sad?" the little spider asked again.

"How could I not be?" asked the turkey. "If you only knew the conversation I've just overheard. It was enough to take anyone's appetite away."

"What conversation was that?" asked the little spider. "What were they talking about?"

"They were talking about me. Can you imagine that? Talking about me! The awful part was what they were saying. That I was nice and plump. That they like me well-roasted. That they want one of my drumsticks. One of MY drumsticks! Can you imagine?"

"Hmmmm . . . " said the little spider. "How curious! How extraordinarily curious!"

"Curious? You call that curious? I call it horrible, terrible, abominable, frightening, scandalous . . . that's what I call it."

"It's just that it's such an interesting coincidence."

"Coincidence? What coincidence?"

"It just so happens that I had a great-grandmother who used to tell me that her great-grandmother had a little pig for a friend, and he also didn't want to get eaten."

"That doesn't seem like such an extraordinary coincidence to me. After all, who *would* like to get eaten?"

“The coincidence is that my great-grandmother told me that her great-grandmother managed to save the life of her friend Wilbur.”

“She managed to save his life? Maybe your great-grandmother did have something interesting to say after all. How did she manage to save his life?”

“My great-grandmother said that her great-grandmother, who was named Charlotte, had thought of a very original way to save Wilbur’s life.”

“A very original way? And what was that?”

“Well, the problem is that I wouldn’t know how to do what my great-grandmother’s great-grandmother did. Because, you see, my great-grandmother’s great-grandmother went to school, and I never did.”

“But what was it that she did to save her friend?”

“She came up with the idea of writing interesting words about Wilbur on her spiderweb. And when people read that Wilbur was ‘radiant’ and ‘some pig,’ they decided not to eat him. But the problem is that, unlike my great-grandmother’s great-grandmother, I never went to school — and I don’t know how to write. So, even if I wanted to write something on my web, I couldn’t do it.”

“Hmmm . . .” said the turkey. “I might have guessed that this coincidence wasn’t going to help solve any problems.”

"Well, I think you're wrong," said the spider. "I've always had a great admiration for my great-grandmother's great-grandmother, so much so that, even though I haven't gone to school as she did, I know that I can figure out a way to help you. And now it would be best for you to let me think. We spiders always think best while we are weaving our webs."

And so the little spider started to spin, and spin, and spin. She spun all morning and she spun all afternoon. That night she was still spinning away under the light of the moon. By the time that morning came the tiny spider had spun an enormous spiderweb.

The turkey, on the other hand, spent the whole day moaning and sighing. That night, his sighs were so loud and so frequent that no one could fall asleep. This went on until the rooster, embarrassed and upset, at last had to say:

"Stop sighing. You're keeping me awake. Don't forget that I have to get up very early to wake up the sun."

The next morning, the turkey returned to the nut tree. He didn't have much confidence that someone as tiny as the spider was going to be able to help him, but she has been the only one who had at least shown an interest in what was happening to him.

"Hello," he said, in a sad and sorry voice.

"Good morning!" said the little spider. "See how right I was? I told you that when we spin and spin, we spiders have time to think. While I spun by the light of the moon, I had a wonderful idea. I know how you can solve your problem."

"Really?" asked the turkey, who was very surprised.

"Of course," said the spider. "They're happy because you're plump, right?"

"Yes, that's what they say."

"Well, then you know what you have to do. Lose weight. Get skinny. Then they won't want to eat you. And, if you get a lot of exercise, those drumsticks of yours, instead of having soft tender meat on them, will have lean, tough muscles that no one will want to eat."

"Really? Are you sure?"

"That's what I think. I already told you that even though I didn't go to school as my great-grandmother's great-grandmother did, I would help you find an answer to your problem. So, let's get started. It's time to exercise! Time to run, time to jump . . . time to fly!"

"Time to fly?" asked the turkey in disbelief. "No one in my family has flown for generations and generations."

"Well then, it must be about time for you to start," said the little spider firmly.

And thus a new life began for the turkey.

Whenever food was brought out to the chicken yard, the turkey would only take a few nibbles. And as for worms, the truth was, they no longer seemed as appetizing as they had before. After all, since the turkey didn't want anyone to eat him, he didn't really want to eat anyone else anymore, either.

In this way, the turkey managed to reduce the amount of food he ate. He also began to exercise both mornings and afternoons. He ran circles around the chicken yard, and jumped from rock to rock.

Bit by bit and day by day, the turkey was in better and better shape.

"You were right," he said to the little spider one morning. "My thighs aren't nearly as soft as they used to be."

"Nor as tasty," said the spider.

"You didn't have to say that," answered the turkey, somewhat upset.

"Well, now it's time for you to start learning to fly."

"To fly?"

"Yes, to fly. Just start by trying to flap up to the lowest branch of the nut tree. Come on now, you can do it."

The turkey began with a running start. Then he flapped his wings frantically, but all that he managed was a high jump.

"You see," said the spider, "with perseverance and effort, you can accomplish anything. Each time, you will be able to fly higher and higher, and I assure you, it's part of my plan."

"Part of your plan? But I thought that your plan was for me to lose weight."

"Well, that was the first part of the plan, but it isn't all of it. You need to keep practicing. Let's see you try it again."

Once again the turkey began with a running start. He flapped his wings and jumped, higher this time than he'd jumped before.

"Very good," said the little spider. "Let's try it once more."

The turkey made another brave attempt. And so it went for the next week. Day after day, Monday and Tuesday, Wednesday and Thursday, Friday and Saturday, the turkey kept practicing and practicing.

He would take off with a running start, flap his wings, and jump a little higher each time.

On Sunday, it rained all day. Monday it rained again. On Tuesday, the little spider sat on her spiderweb and observed how, during this last week of November, more activity than ever was taking place inside the house.

All of the rugs had been shaken out. The curtains had been taken down and then hung back up again. The porch had been decorated with pumpkins and brightly colored ears of corn.

Many cars had arrived, bringing family members from far away.

The little spider observed all of this with great attention and interest from her post high up on a branch of the nut tree.

“I think that today you should exercise more than ever,” she said to the turkey.

And then she began to cheer him on.

“Let’s start with ten laps around the chicken yard.”

When the turkey had finished the laps, the spider did not give him time to rest, but instead pushed him further:

“Now let’s try flapping ten times up to the lowest branch.”

That afternoon, just as the spider had feared, the cook came out of the house and appeared very intent on finding someone.

"The time that you have been preparing for has now arrived," said the spider to the turkey. "I believe you need to get ready to run. This time, run to the fence . . . and remember, it's no higher than the lowest branch of the nut tree."

Until that moment, the turkey had not understood what it was that the spider had in mind.

All of a sudden he heard a voice which said:

"Ah! There's the turkey! Let's grab him now; it's time to start dressing him for dinner."

For the turkey, those words were the signal which announced the beginning of his race.

He set off at top speed flapping his wings as hard as he could.

And remembering that the fence was no higher than the lowest branch of the nut tree, he made a great leap and disappeared into the forest. He has lived there ever since, eating a vegetarian diet and exercising faithfully every day.